GPJC
1/20

STAR WARS
THE RISE OF SKYWALKER
WARS

THE GALACTIC GUIDE

STAR
THE RISE OF SKYWALKER
WARS

THE GALACTIC GUIDE

Written by Matt Jones

CONTENTS

INTRODUCTION

About a year has passed since the Battle of Crait. The peaceful galactic government named the New Republic has been destroyed. Supreme Leader Kylo Ren and the evil First Order reign over most of the galaxy. Only Rey, Finn, Poe, and the other brave heroes of the Resistance stand against their complete rule of the galaxy.

THE RESISTANCE

General Leia Organa leads a small military force named the Resistance. These brave rebels have sworn to restore peace and democracy to the galaxy. But first, they must defeat the First Order!

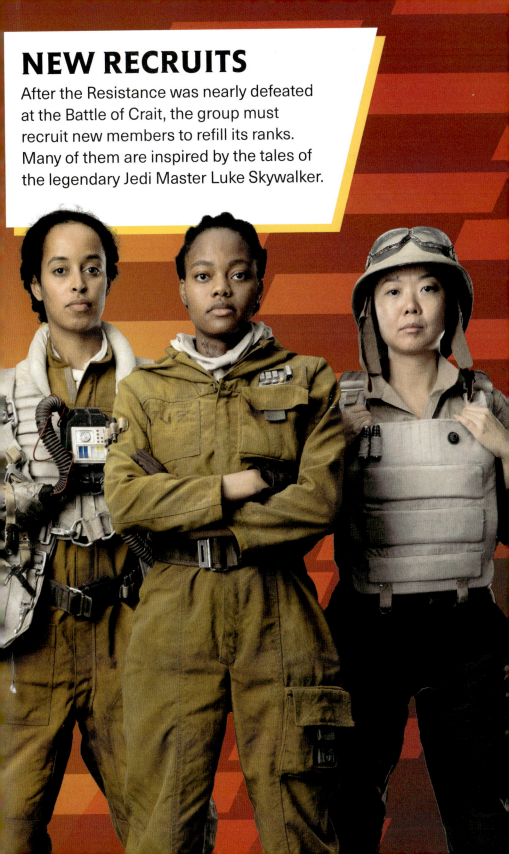

NEW RECRUITS

After the Resistance was nearly defeated at the Battle of Crait, the group must recruit new members to refill its ranks. Many of them are inspired by the tales of the legendary Jedi Master Luke Skywalker.

AJAN KLOSS

This uninhabited, jungle planet is the perfect hideout for General Organa's Resistance forces. This beautiful world is full of wildlife so it is strong in the Force and an ideal place for Rey to train to be a Jedi.

RESISTANCE BASE

Leia has known for decades that Ajan Kloss might make a suitable location for a base. Her troops have not been there long, and they are still building the site. In the meantime, Leia's command ship, the *Tantive IV*, is a temporary alternative to use as a base.

 LEIA ORGANA

Resistance leader

Leia Organa is a noble and legendary general. For years, she was worried about the threat of the First Order, so she created the Resistance to protect peace in the galaxy.

Things you need to know about Leia

1 Her brother, Jedi Master Luke Skywalker, started teaching Leia how to use the Force after the Battle of Endor.

2 Leia has reclaimed the *Tantive IV*, a ship she used years ago when fighting the evil Empire.

3 She has been passing on her wisdom to the younger members of the Resistance.

4 When the Resistance hears of a new danger, she sends her best troops on a mission to find out more information.

REY

Brave warrior

Rey is a Jedi with a mighty reputation. She is determined to fight the First Order. Rey lives on the planet Ajan Kloss with her friends in the Resistance. She is training to improve her abilities with the Force.

Things you need to know about Rey

1 General Leia Organa has passed on her own Jedi knowledge to Rey.

2 Rey has a small library of ancient Jedi texts that she uses to study the ways of the Force.

3 Rey keeps many mechanical tools in her workbench at the Resistance base.

4 Rey develops her Force skills with training remotes—small droids with built-in blasters. They are much like the ones Luke once used in his training.

15

SKILLED MECHANIC

Rey has spent most of her life scavenging equipment and repairing it, in order to sell it on. She still enjoys fixing things.

REBUILT LIGHTSABER

Rey's lightsaber was broken in two during a duel with Kylo Ren. Using the Force and the knowledge in her Jedi books, Rey has now repaired it.

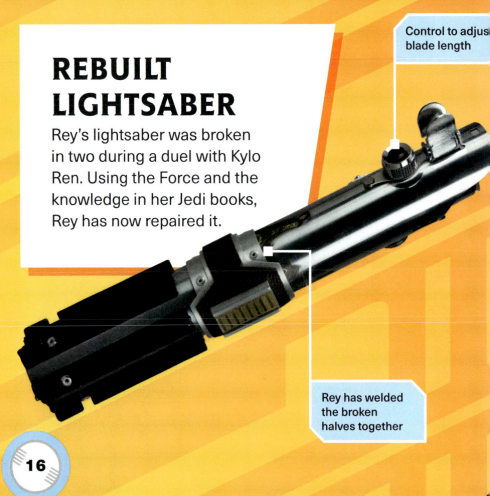

Control to adjust blade length

Rey has welded the broken halves together

Did you know?

Each lightsaber has a kyber crystal inside it. These special crystals power the blades.

Laser cannon

X-WING

X-wings are dependable fighters in the Resistance fleet. Each X-wing has four powerful laser cannons.

RESISTANCE STARSHIPS

After many ships were destroyed in the Battle of D'Qar, the Resistance has been slowly increasing its number of starfighters. Unfortunately, the group only has a few dozen ships—not enough for a fleet!

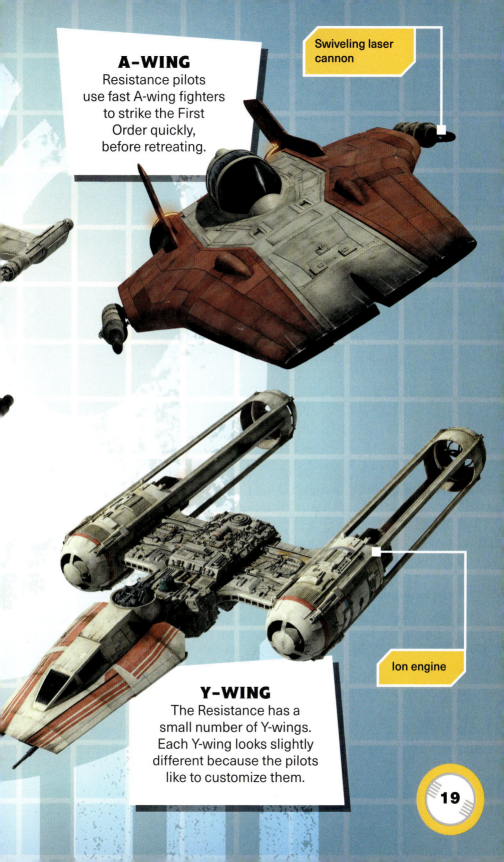

A-WING
Resistance pilots use fast A-wing fighters to strike the First Order quickly, before retreating.

Y-WING
The Resistance has a small number of Y-wings. Each Y-wing looks slightly different because the pilots like to customize them.

20

 # FINN

Courageous hero

Finn used to be a First Order stormtrooper named FN-2187. Now he is a loyal member of the First Order's enemy, the Resistance. Finn is a brave and capable fighter. He uses his expert knowledge to help the Resistance.

Things you need to know about Finn

1 Thanks to his stormtrooper training, Finn can use a variety of weapons.

2 The First Order's officers want to capture Finn. They are outraged that he dared to betray them.

3 Finn used to wear his friend Poe's jacket, but he now has one of his own.

4 Over the past year, Finn has become closer friends with Rey.

SMART SOLDIER

Finn is eager to learn more so he can fight the First Order to the best of his abilities. He has been working hard to hone his piloting and language skills since the Battle of Crait.

FIRM FRIENDS

Finn and Poe first met when they worked together to escape Kylo Ren's Star Destroyer, the *Finalizer*. They have become even better friends since then.

Standard Resistance blaster

Flight jacket with sleeves removed

23

POE DAMERON

Daring pilot

Poe Dameron is one of the greatest pilots in the galaxy. He joined the Resistance and has risen through the ranks to become a strong and inspiring leader.

Things you need to know about Poe

1 Poe has a new orange-and-white X-wing, which is the same model as his old, destroyed starfighter, *Black One*.

2 He has sometimes struggled with being responsible, but has learned much from his mentor, General Organa.

3 Poe used to be a smuggler, but he turned his back on that way of life and joined the New Republic Navy.

4 When Poe was a child, his mom, a rebel pilot named Shara Bey, taught him how to pilot her A-wing.

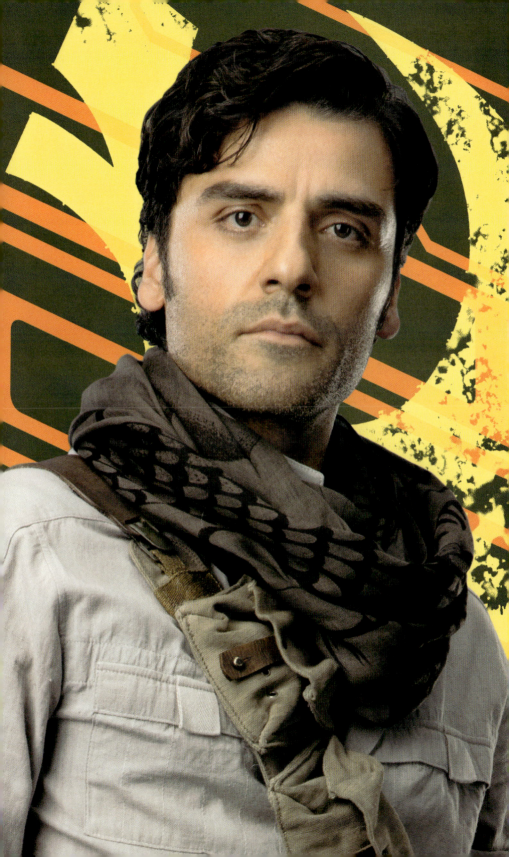

BB-8

Helpful droid

BB-8 is a smart and loyal astromech. He is very handy on missions because he carries lots of tools inside his round body. BB-8 joined the Resistance with Poe after their time in the New Republic.

Things you need to know about BB-8

1 BB-8 is a modern droid built by Industrial Automaton, the same company that makes R2 units.

2 Nowadays he mainly keeps Rey company on Ajan Kloss.

3 BB-8 has been separated from Poe before. He once went on a spy mission to the Colossus fueling station.

4 He is more than happy to look after his new droid friend, D-O.

CHEWBACCA

Honorable Wookiee

Chewbacca, or Chewie to his friends, is a towering Wookiee from Kashyyyk. He thinks of Rey, Finn, and Poe as his family. Chewie will do anything to help and protect them.

Things you need to know about Chewie

1 Chewie is more than 200 years old, but he shows few signs of aging.

2 He recently lent the *Millennium Falcon* ship to the former pirate Hondo Ohnaka.

3 Chewie keeps spare ammunition and repair tools in his carry pouch.

4 He joins the other Resistance heroes on their mission to learn more about the Sith planet Exegol.

5 Chewie has been playing lots of dejarik (a holographic chess game) and is now very good at it.

R2-D2

Old ally

For decades, R2-D2 has been loyal to the Skywalker family and has helped them in their fights against evil. The astromech droid now works as Poe Dameron's copilot on missions.

Things you need to know about R2-D2

1 Unlike many droids, R2-D2 has never had his mind wiped, so he remembers lots of useful information.

2 R2-D2 has been talking to BB-8 to learn how best to support Poe when he is in the cockpit.

3 He has a copy of the old Death Star plans in his system, which may come in handy.

4 R2-D2 even holds backups of his friend C-3PO's memories.

C-3PO

Golden droid

C-3PO is a very talkative and polite protocol droid. Protocol droids know many different languages and can help people across the galaxy understand one another. C-3PO has been a member of the Resistance since it was created.

Things you need to know about C-3PO

1 C-3PO was built years ago by Anakin Skywalker, the father of Leia Organa.

2 He has set up a network of droid spies to keep an eye on the First Order.

3 C-3PO knows more than seven million languages.

4 He is very good at math and can figure out how likely it is that an event might happen.

RESISTANCE COMMANDERS

The Resistance may be a tiny group compared to the vast ranks of the First Order. However, its members include some of the brightest and bravest people in the galaxy!

ROSE TICO

Rose Tico joined the Resistance as a mechanic. Now, Rose is in charge of the group's engineers. She thinks up clever ideas to beat the First Order's technology.

KAYDEL CONNIX

Kaydel Connix is very good at organizing troops and equipment, so she helps set up the base on Ajan Kloss. Kaydel has also become friends with Rose Tico and Beaumont Kin.

BEAUMONT KIN

New recruit Beaumont Kin used to be a professor in a school. He enjoyed studying the history of the Sith and the Jedi. Now, Beaumont helps Rey translate her ancient Jedi books.

RESISTANCE COMMANDERS
(CONTINUED)

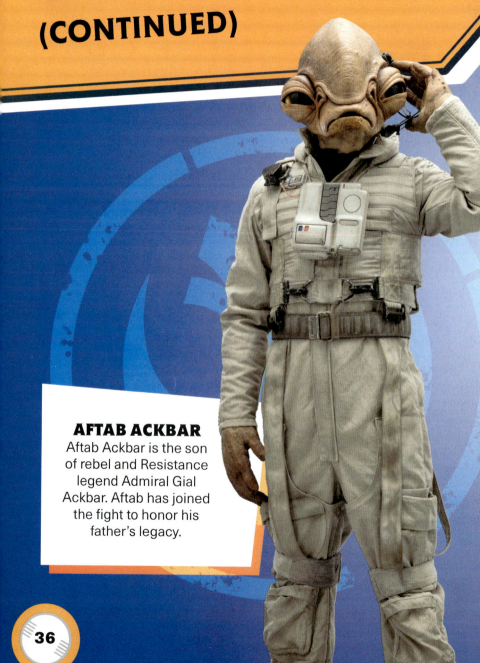

AFTAB ACKBAR

Aftab Ackbar is the son of rebel and Resistance legend Admiral Gial Ackbar. Aftab has joined the fight to honor his father's legacy.

LARMA D'ACY

Larma provides expert tactical knowledge to the Resistance. She holds the rank of Commander and proudly serves alongside her wife, Tyce, who is a starfighter pilot.

SNAP WEXLEY

As a teenager, Snap fought against the Empire. Decades later, he is one of the Resistance's best pilots, especially on spying missions.

MAZ KANATA

Force-sensitive Maz Kanata does not join the Resistance in battle. She remains on Ajan Kloss to offer her wise words to her comrades.

MILLENNIUM FALCON

The Resistance would have been destroyed if Rey and Chewie hadn't come to the rescue in the *Falcon* during the Battle of Crait. After spending a brief amount of time on Batuu, the legendary ship is now back in the hands of the Resistance.

Top hatch comes in handy on certain missions

New circular rectenna

STILL GOT IT

Poe Dameron is still getting used to piloting the *Falcon*. Much like Han Solo before him, Poe pushes the ship to its limits.

WHICH HERO ARE YOU MOST LIKE?

From Leia Organa to BB-8, the Resistance is full of inspiring heroes. Take the quiz to find out which one you are most like!

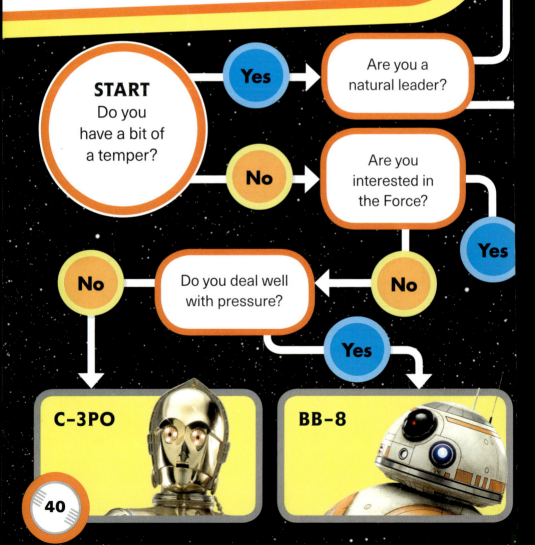

START
Do you have a bit of a temper?

Yes → Are you a natural leader?

No → Are you interested in the Force?

No → Do you deal well with pressure?

Yes

No → C-3PO

Yes → BB-8

Is flying one of your favorite activities?

Yes → POE

No → LEIA

Yes

Do you feel at home in a forest?

No

Yes → CHEWBACCA

No

Are you good at repairing things?

No

Yes → R2-D2

FINN

REY

THE FIRST ORDER

The First Order has taken over much of the galaxy and is firmly under Supreme Leader Kylo Ren's control. This ruthless group attacks anyone or any planets that resist its rule.

RETURN TO ORDER

For years, the First Order had to keep its true strength hidden. However, its leaders do not have to worry anymore since they have defeated the New Republic.

 KYLO REN

Supreme Leader

The scary leader of the First Order, Kylo Ren is strong with the dark side of the Force. This ferocious warrior will stop at nothing to track down the secrets of the Sith.

Things you need to know about Kylo

1 Kylo often sends his scary Knights of Ren to hunt down anyone who challenges his rule.

2 He could repair his lightsaber to make it more stable, but he likes how the jagged blade looks.

3 Kylo's parents, Leia Organa and Han Solo, named him Ben, but he chose a new name when he turned evil.

4 Kylo is experiencing mysterious Force visions. He is desperate to find out what they mean!

FEROCIOUS WARRIOR

Kylo Ren is a skilled fighter, whether he is on the ground or in space. He learned how to use the Force and how to wield a lightsaber from his uncle, Jedi Master Luke Skywalker— and then used these skills against him.

GREAT PILOT

Like his father, Han Solo, Kylo is an expert pilot. Kylo flies in a modified TIE whisper starfighter, which has been adapted so it is incredibly fast and stealthy.

Broken helmet repaired by loyal Sith follower

Did you know?
Kylo starts wearing his helmet again after he becomes Supreme Leader.

Dark side Force users prefer red blades

KNIGHTS OF REN

The Knights of Ren are a small band of warriors, led by Kylo Ren. They all wear masks to make themselves look menacing. The Knights have limited, untrained Force powers, but they are still very dangerous.

Fearsome scythe is Vicrul's preferred weapon

VICRUL
Without realizing he is even doing it, Vicrul uses the Force to make his foes more terrified of him!

Customized arm cannon has a built-in flamethrower

CARDO
This creative Knight enjoys causing lots of chaos in battle.

War club packs a heavy punch

USHAR
Ushar's mask has special breathing filters, which suggests he might be an alien.

KNIGHTS OF REN
(CONTINUED)

Did you know?

Kylo Ren had to pass a test given by Supreme Leader Snoke in order to become the boss of the Knights of Ren.

TRUDGEN

Trudgen is a keen collector and has many trophies from his past missions.

Rifle has many different firing settings

KURUK
This Knight is a bit of a loner. He prefers ranged weapons, and is the pilot of the team's ship.

Helmet looks like a creepy smile

AP´LEK
Ap'lek is a sneaky Knight who prefers to trap his targets.

FIRST ORDER COMMANDERS

Kylo Ren has set up a small group of high-ranking First Order military officers. Known as the Supreme Council, these experts offer Kylo guidance on how to shape the First Order's future.

GENERAL HUX

General Armitage Hux never liked Kylo Ren, even before Kylo became the Supreme Leader. Hux has been demoted in the new regime and lacks any real authority.

Mouth twisted into a disapproving sneer

ALLEGIANT GENERAL PRYDE

Pryde is a former Imperial officer, who once witnessed the evil Sith Darth Vader in action. Pryde later joins the First Order and is given an important job by Supreme Leader Kylo Ren.

Did you know?

Pryde is in command of the *Steadfast,* a First Order Star Destroyer.

FIRST ORDER TROOPS

The First Order is full of passionate believers. They think that they are the rightful rulers of the galaxy. The troops even believe that the First Order's strict laws are helping the galaxy's citizens.

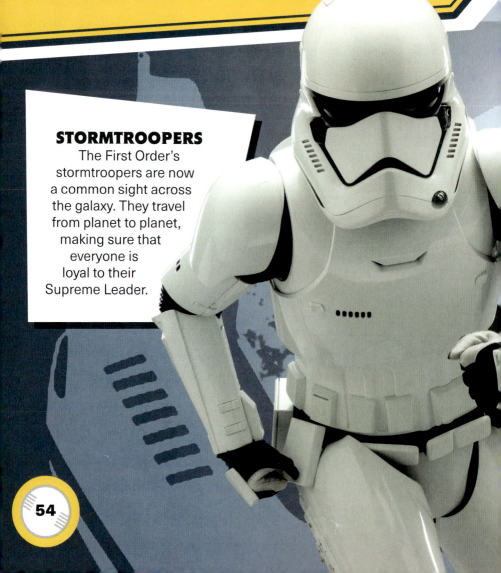

STORMTROOPERS

The First Order's stormtroopers are now a common sight across the galaxy. They travel from planet to planet, making sure that everyone is loyal to their Supreme Leader.

TIE PILOTS
These skilled pilots fly a range of TIE fighters into battle against their targets.

FLEET PERSONNEL
Fleet personnel make sure that the First Order's ships do not break down.

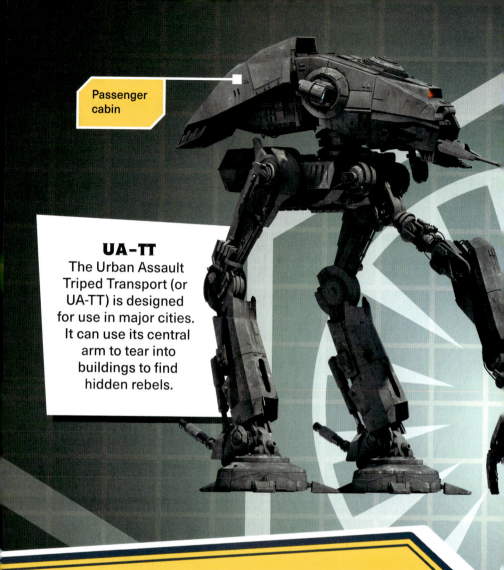

Passenger cabin

UA-TT
The Urban Assault Triped Transport (or UA-TT) is designed for use in major cities. It can use its central arm to tear into buildings to find hidden rebels.

FIRST ORDER VEHICLES

The First Order is always working with its engineers to create even better vehicles. The starships, walkers, and speeders are often tailored to specific conditions.

TIE WHISPER

The TIE whisper is one of the newest types of First Order starfighters. It has a hyperdrive, which allows it to travel across the galaxy.

Two powerful laser cannons

TREADSPEEDER

Specially trained pilots use these agile speeders to chase down their targets. The speeders also have space to carry a jet trooper, who can soar into the sky to provide covering fire.

MUSTAFAR

Darth Vader built a castle on the fiery, volcanic planet Mustafar. The planet has recently started to cool down, which has attracted some new residents.

ALAZMEC CULTISTS
The Alazmec cultists are devoted followers of the deceased Darth Vader. They have settled on Mustafar where they protect and nurture the Corvax Fen—a marshy area that survives in the middle of the lava.

Did you know?

Kylo Ren wants to visit the ruins of Darth Vader's castle. The Alazmec cultists try, and fail, to stop him.

THE SITH

After the death of Darth Sidious on the Death Star II, Luke Skywalker believed the Sith to be extinct. While the Sith Lords may have died, a group loyal to the Sith survived in secret. These evil people are desperate to conquer the galaxy.

FIRST ORDER CONNECTIONS

Not even Supreme Leader Kylo Ren knew about these loyalists, but a few people in the First Order were aware of them. Kylo later discovers the loyalists and learns that they want him to become a new Sith Lord.

EXEGOL

Exegol is a barren world that is hidden deep within the Unknown Regions of the galaxy. For more than 1,000 years it was a power base for the Sith Lords. Now, the Sith loyalists keep their army and a fleet of ships lying in wait here.

SITH WAYFINDER

It is nearly impossible to travel across the Unknown Regions, so the Sith Lords used devices named Sith Wayfinders to reach Exegol. These pieces of technology look like Sith Holocrons (data storage devices) and can be connected to a ship's nav computer.

SITH TROOPS

The Sith cultists on Exegol have been secretly building an army dedicated to retaking the galaxy. These troops are not Force-sensitive, but they are even better trained and equipped than the members of the First Order military.

SITH TROOPERS
Clad in crimson armor, the Sith troopers have been brainwashed to be completely loyal to the Sith leader. The very best of these troops are named Sovereign Protectors.

SITH JET TROOPERS

Taking to the skies, the Sith jet troopers protect their planet from enemies. They are speedy and able to dodge enemy weapon fire.

SITH FLEET TECHNICIANS

These smart technicians work hard to keep the fearsome Sith Star Destroyers in perfect condition.

SITH STARSHIPS

For decades, the Sith cultists have been creating new ships and preparing to unleash them on the galaxy. They are now ready to launch their terrifying weapons and destroy anyone who stands in their way.

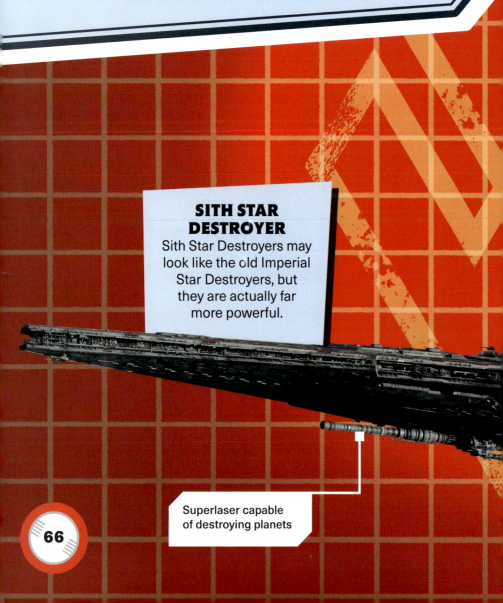

SITH STAR DESTROYER

Sith Star Destroyers may look like the old Imperial Star Destroyers, but they are actually far more powerful.

Superlaser capable of destroying planets

Laser cannon nestled between the wings

TIE DAGGER
These fast and powerful TIE fighters are named after their dagger-like wings.

HEROES' MISSION

When the Resistance hears that there is a Sith fleet about to attack the galaxy, General Organa assembles her best troops. Rey, Finn, Poe, BB-8, Chewbacca, and C-3PO are tasked with finding out more information about Exegol—a Sith world that Luke once tried to find. They begin their hunt where Luke's ended: on the planet Pasaana.

PASAANA

Desert planets are widely believed to be lifeless worlds, but Pasaana is not one of them. The world is actually full of different life-forms and even has underground gardens.

PARTY PEOPLE

The local Aki-Aki people are friendly and hold a massive party once every two years named the Festival of the Ancestors. They store lots of food and drink for each celebration. Many offworlders come to visit and join in.

True or False?

Luke Skywalker never
visited Pasaana.

A: False. Luke Skywalker visited
Pasaana to try and find forgotten
Jedi and Sith knowledge.

SPEEDER CHASE

After the Resistance heroes are spotted on Pasaana, the First Order sends a patrol to capture them. Poe finds a couple of local speeders, which the heroes use to escape quickly!

Grain ready for market

Main thruster

TRANSPORT SKIMMER
Rey, Chewbacca, and BB-8 ride on this transport. While Rey pilots the basic, unarmored vehicle, BB-8 and Chewie try to stop their pursuers.

Steering vane

LOADER SKIMMER
Poe drives this fast skimmer with Finn and C-3PO as passengers. Finn fires on the attacking jet troopers while C-3PO panics over the fact that the troops can fly.

Jetpack built into armor

JET TROOPERS
The First Order trains a number of troopers in aerial combat. They wear jetpacks and can attack their foes from above.

LANDO CALRISSIAN

Living legend

Lando Calrissian's name is known throughout the galaxy. He has been a famous smuggler, a former Baron of Cloud City, and even a Rebel Alliance general. This daring hero is always ready to fight against evil.

Things you need to know about Lando

1 He was a loving father to his daughter, until she was kidnapped by the First Order.

2 Lando still has many contacts from his days as a smuggler, who would come to his aid if he requested it.

3 Years ago, Lando traveled with his friend Luke Skywalker to discover if the Sith survived.

4 Lando decided to settle on Pasaana and live among the friendly Aki-Aki people.

5 To protect himself and the Aki-Aki, Lando wears a disguise on Pasaana and is known only as the Hermit.

VEXIS

The vexis is a scary, snakelike creature that is native to the desert planet Pasaana. It lives underground, building tunnels that it can use in the future and hunting for prey.

Tough armor plates

Multiple eyes are not very strong

Teeth are incredibly sharp

Did you know?

The vexis' skin releases oils that strengthen the tunnels that it creates.

Did you know?

The First Order raids Kijimi City, kidnapping its children. The kids will be trained as stormtroopers.

KIJIMI

The mountainous, cold world of Kijimi was never under the control of the New Republic, and it is a haven for criminals. However, the First Order's recent visits means that Kijimi's lawless days might be numbered.

CHILLY CITY

Kijimi City used to be a former Dai Bendu monastery. Visitors have to wrap up in warm clothes because it is freezing all year round!

ZORII BLISS

Tough leader

Zorii Bliss joined the Spice Runners gang when she was young, but now she is in charge. Her pirate gang is famous for its criminal activities, and operates out of her lawless homeworld of Kijimi.

Things you need to know about Zorii

1 Zorii is a skilled gunslinger, who wields a pair of E-851 blaster pistols.

2 Her bronze helmet contains technology that aids her in battle—whether she is on the ground or in the cockpit of her Y-wing starfighter.

3 Her acrobatic grace in combat comes from her dance training.

4 She used to be friends with Poe Dameron, who was also a Spice Runner until he joined the New Republic.

D-O

Friendly droid

D-O is a cute and kind machine who the Resistance heroes meet during their mission. He becomes friends with BB-8 and follows him wherever he goes.

Things you need to know about D-O

1 D-O once belonged to a Sith assassin named Ochi of Bestoon.

2 He may have had a wicked owner, but this little droid is not evil at all.

3 D-O is not sure how old he is, but he was built at least 14 years ago.

4 D-O sometimes becomes quite nervous, but BB-8 can calm him down.

KEF BIR

Kef Bir is one of many moons that orbits the giant gas planet Endor. This moon is covered in oceans, with some grassy islands emerging from the waters. Herds of wild orbak creatures live here.

THE SKY FELL

When the Death Star II was destroyed by the Rebel Alliance, some of the wreckage from the battle station crashed onto Kef Bir. Surprisingly, Kef Bir was not destroyed, but unfortunately the waters surrounding the wreckage have suffered from toxic pollution.

Did you know?

This oceanic moon is named Kef Bir by the Ewoks, who live on the nearby Forest Moon of Endor.

JANNAH

First Order mutineer

The First Order kidnapped Jannah when she was young and forced her to become a stormtooper. She joined Company 77, a training group of stormtroopers. Company 77 rebelled when First Order leaders ordered it to attack civilians.

Things you need to know about Jannah

1 Jannah and the rest of Company 77 ran away and settled on Kef Bir, where they are hiding from the First Order.

2 After Company 77 mutinied, Jannah rose through the ranks to become the leader of the group.

3 Jannah is a skilled engineer. She created her powered bow by reusing parts from blaster rifles.

4 She has a natural ability to make her comrades trust and follow her.

ORBAKS

Orbaks are strong and tough animals found on multiple planets across the galaxy. The members of Company 77 have tamed a herd of orbaks and use them to travel around Kef Bir.

FORTEN

Forten is in charge of caring for all of Company 77's orbaks.

88

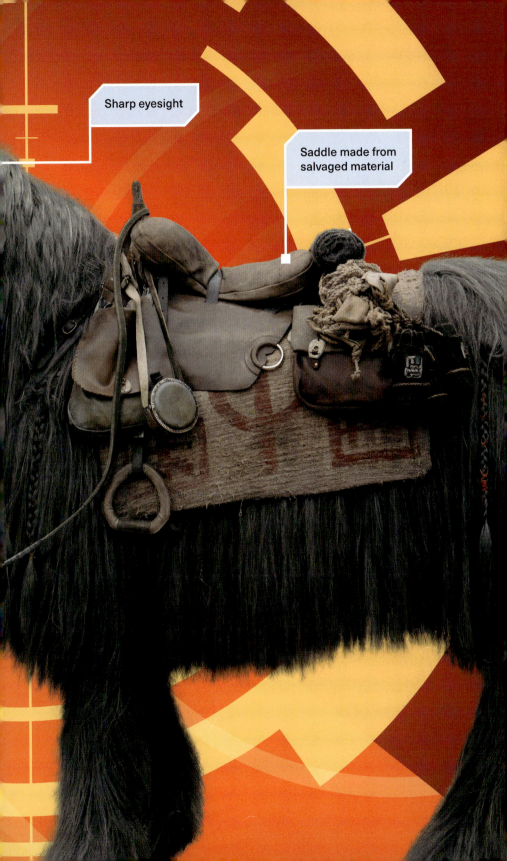

WHICH PLANET WOULD YOU LIKE TO VISIT?

The galaxy is an incredible place. There are so many worlds to visit. Where would be your ideal vacation spot?

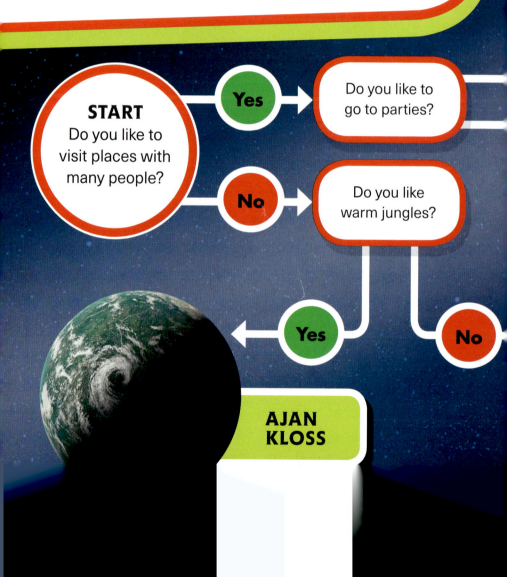

START
Do you like to visit places with many people?

Yes → Do you like to go to parties?

No → Do you like warm jungles?

Yes

No

AJAN KLOSS

PASAANA

EXEGOL

Yes

No → Do you like learning about Sith history? → **Yes**

No

KIJIMI

GLOSSARY

cultist
A person who believes in an unusual religion.

demote
When a boss changes a worker's rank to a lower position.

Empire
An evil group that was in power 30 years ago and was defeated by the Rebel Alliance.

ferocious
Very angry or violent.

gunslinger
A person who is very good at using blasters.

Imperial
Belonging to the Empire.

Jedi
A noble group of people who use the Force to protect others and keep peace.

loyalist

Someone who believes in a group or cause and follows it faithfully.

mutineer

Someone who disagrees with the actions of a group they belong to and decides to rebel.

New Republic

A group that peacefully ruled the galaxy after the defeat of the Empire.

Rebel Alliance

An army of brave people that defeated the Empire.

scavenging

The act of going through trash to see if anything can be reused.

Sith

An ancient group of wicked people who use the dark side of the Force and want to rule over the galaxy.

Sith Lord

A leader of the Sith.

"We're all in this to the end."

Finn

Penguin
Random
House

Edited by Ruth Amos and Matt Jones
Senior Designer Clive Savage
Project Art Editor Jon Hall
Designer Chris Gould
Creative Technical Support Steve Crozier,
Adam Brackenbury, and Tom Morse
Pre-Production Producer Marc Staples
Senior Producer Mary Slater
Managing Editor Sarah Harland
Managing Art Editor Vicky Short
Publisher Julie Ferris
Art Director Lisa Lanzarini

For Lucasfilm
Senior Editor Brett Rector
Creative Director Michael Siglain
Art Director Troy Alders
Story Group James Waugh, Pablo Hidalgo,
Leland Chee, and Matt Martin
Asset Management Gabrielle Levenson
Tim Mapp, Bryce Pinkos, and Erik Sanchez

First American Edition, 2019
Published in the United States by DK Publishing
1450 Broadway, Suite 801, New York, NY 10018

Page design copyright © 2019 Dorling Kindersley Limited
DK, a Division of Penguin Random House LLC

19 20 21 22 23 10 9 8 7 6 5 4 3 2 1
001–311517–Dec/2019

A catalog record for this book is available from
the Library of Congress.
ISBN 978-1-4654-7906-8

DK books are available at special discounts when
purchased in bulk for sales promotions, premiums,
fund-raising, or educational use. For details,
contact:
DK Publishing Special Markets, 1450 Broadway,
Suite 801, New York, NY 10018
SpecialSales@dk.com

Printed and bound in the USA

A WORLD OF IDEAS:
SEE ALL THERE IS TO KNOW

www.DK.com
www.starwars.com

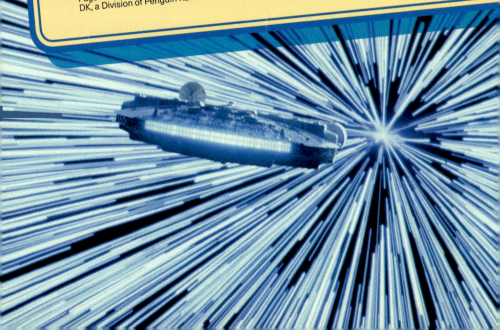